P9-DHJ-425

The *Secret* Shortcut

by MARK TEAGUE

SCHOLASTIC INC.
New York   Toronto   London   Auckland   Sydney
Mexico City   New Delhi   Hong Kong

**For Peter
and Timothy**

No part of this publication may be reproduced in whole or in part, or stored in a
retrieval system, or transmitted in any form or by any means, electronic,
mechanical, photocopying, recording, or otherwise, without written permission
of the publisher. For information regarding permission, write to
Scholastic Inc., Attention: Permissions Department,
555 Broadway, New York, NY 10012.

ISBN 0-439-11091-2

Copyright © 1996 by Mark Teague. All rights reserved.
Published by Scholastic Inc.
SCHOLASTIC and associated logos are trademarks and/or
registered trademarks of Scholastic Inc.

25 24 23 22   13 14 15/0

Printed in the U.S.A.   08

First Scholastic Trade paperback printing, September 1999

The text type is Usherwood Bold, set by WLCR New York.
The illustrations for this book were painted in acrylic.

ON Monday, Wendell and Floyd were late for school.

They had nearly been captured by space creatures, they told their teacher.

"Ridiculous," said Ms. Gernsblatt, and she warned them not to let it happen again.

But Tuesday was no better. Pirates were loose in the neighborhood. It was sheer bad luck, Wendell and Floyd explained, when they showed up late for school.

"Preposterous!" said Ms. Gernsblatt.

And on Wednesday, even though Wendell and Floyd left early, a plague of frogs made them late once again.

"Absurd!" cried their teacher. "I'm warning you — be here on time tomorrow — or else! And no more crazy excuses!"

"There's got to be a way to get to school on time," said Wendell. "We'll just have to leave earlier."

Floyd arrived at Wendell's house so early the next morning that the sun was barely up, and Wendell was still in his pajamas.

"I've got an idea," said Wendell as he quickly got dressed. "We'll follow my secret shortcut and get to school even sooner."

"Shortcut?" asked Floyd. "I didn't know there were any good shortcuts to school."

"This is the secretest shortcut of all," said Wendell. "In fact, I invented it myself."

He led Floyd up the alley by the Oolicks' backyard, then down a culvert, over a fence, and through a dense thicket of blackberry vines.

Then they scrambled over some boulders, down a steep bank, and across a narrow stream.

"This is some shortcut," said Floyd.

"Relax," said Wendell. "We'll be there in a minute."

But the forest became thicker and darker. Soon it was hung with vines. The screeches of strange jungle animals echoed all around.

"Maybe we took a wrong turn," said Floyd.

"I'm pretty sure the school is right up ahead," Wendell told him.

But the jungle only grew wilder. And when the boys finally came to a trail, it didn't lead straight to the school, as they had hoped. Instead, it meandered through quicksand swamps and past large, sleeping crocodiles . . .

and across a deep, rocky gorge.

It began to get late.
"This is going to be hard to explain," said Floyd.
They stood in a small clearing.
"I have an idea," said Wendell. "We'll climb a tree and see
if we can spot the school."

They chose the biggest, tallest tree they could find and climbed
all the way to the top.

"Do you see the school?" asked Wendell.

"I don't even see the town," said Floyd.

They watched some monkeys playing in the treetops.

"I have another idea," said Wendell.

"What is it?" asked Floyd. He was getting tired of Wendell's ideas.

"We'll swing from these vines just like the monkeys," said Wendell.
"That way we'll travel much faster."

Soon they were swinging from vine to vine.
"This isn't bad," shouted Floyd. "I'll bet we're making good time."
"I knew this shortcut would work out," Wendell crowed.
But at that moment they ran out of vines.

The boys landed — *plop, plop* — in a giant puddle of mud.
"Now what do we do?" asked Floyd.
"I don't know," said Wendell. "I'm out of ideas."
They sat in the puddle and thought about all the trouble
they were going to be in. "Ms. Gernsblatt will never believe
this story," said Wendell.
"It is sort of crazy," said Floyd.
Just then, from far away, they heard a school bell ring.

"Did you hear that?" cried Wendell. "That was the first bell. We can still make it if we run!"

They ran until the jungle gave way to forest, and the forest became woods, and then they scurried through the Mortleys' backyard and up the hill to the school. They flew through the door of Ms. Gernsblatt's room and landed squishily in their seats just as the late bell rang.

"Well, you made it," said their teacher. "And just in time. But how on earth did you get so muddy just walking to school?"

Floyd looked at Wendell. Wendell looked at Floyd.

"On second thought," said Ms. Gernsblatt, "maybe you'd better not say."

During recess, Wendell and Floyd sat in the sun to give the mud a chance to dry.

"At least we finally got to school on time," said Wendell.

"That's the main thing," Floyd agreed.

And in fact it was quite a while before they were late to school again.

Even so, they never did find a really *good* shortcut.